THE *DIARY OF A WIMPY KID* SERIES

1 Diary of a Wimpy Kid
2 Rodrick Rules
3 The Last Straw
4 Dog Days
5 The Ugly Truth
6 Cabin Fever
7 The Third Wheel
8 Hard Luck
9 The Long Haul
10 Old School
11 Double Down
12 The Getaway
13 The Meltdown

ALSO BY JEFF KINNEY

The Wimpy Kid Do-It-Yourself Book

The Wimpy Kid Movie Diary

The Wimpy Kid Movie Diary: The Next Chapter

Diary of an Awesome Friendly Kid: Rowley Jefferson's Journal

DIARY
of a
Wimpy Kid
THE MELTDOWN

by Jeff Kinney

AMULET BOOKS

New York

Library of Congress Control Number: 2018038582

ISBN 978-1-4197-4199-9

Book design by Jeff Kinney
Cover design by Chad W. Beckerman and Jeff Kinney

Printed and bound in U.S.A.
16 15 14 13 12 11 10 9 8 7 6

Amulet Books are available at special discounts when purchased in quantity for premiums and promotions as well as fundraising or educational use. Special editions can also be created to specification. For details, contact specialsales@abramsbooks.com or the address below.

Amulet Books® is a registered trademark of Harry N. Abrams, Inc.

ABRAMS The Art of Books
195 Broadway, New York, NY 10007
abramsbooks.com

TO DEB

JANUARY

<u>Monday</u>

Everybody in my neighborhood is outside today enjoying the warm weather and sunshine. Well, everyone except ME. It's kind of hard to enjoy a heat wave when it's the middle of the WINTER.

People are calling this "wacky weather," but it just doesn't feel right. Maybe I'm old-fashioned, but I think it should be cold in the winter and hot in the SUMMER.

I've heard the whole PLANET is warming up, and that human beings are the reason. But don't blame ME, because I just GOT here.

If the world IS getting hotter, I just hope it doesn't happen too FAST. Because if things keep up at THIS rate, I'll be riding a camel to high school.

They say the ice caps are melting and the sea is rising, so I've been trying to convince Mom and Dad to buy a house higher up on our hill. But they just don't seem all that concerned.

It kind of makes me nervous that I'm the only one in my family worried about this stuff. Because if we don't do something about the situation SOON, we're gonna wish we DID.

It's not just the rising sea levels I'm nervous about. Those ice caps have been around for millions of years, and there could be things buried inside of them that should STAY that way.

I saw a movie about a caveman who got frozen in ice, and when it melted thousands of years later he was still ALIVE. I don't know if that kind of thing could actually happen in real life, but if there ARE unfrozen cavemen walking around these days, the night janitor at my school might be one of them.

SPLOP

If we DO figure a way out of this climate mess, it's probably gonna be someone from MY generation who solves it. That's why I'm always nice to the SMART kids, because THEY'RE the ones who are gonna save our butts.

NERD!

SHOVE

Whatever the answer is, I guarantee you TECHNOLOGY is gonna be the key.

Grown-ups are always saying that too much technology is BAD for kids, but I say the more the BETTER.

In fact, as soon as I can afford one of those high-tech toilets that learns all your habits, I'm gonna get the most expensive model.

Some people worry that one day we'll lose control of our technology and robots will take OVER.

Well, if that happens, I'm gonna make sure I'm on THEIR side.

I've actually been PREPARING for when the robots take over by sucking up to the appliances in my house.

So when there's a giant robot/human war in the future, I'll be patting myself on the back for thinking ahead.

My brother Rodrick says that in the future, people will have robot body parts, and we'll all be CYBORGS.

Well, I hope I don't have to wait too long for that, because if I could buy myself a pair of robot legs, I could get a half hour of extra sleep each morning.

I guess we don't really know what's gonna happen in the future. And you could drive yourself CRAZY worrying about it.

Even if we solve all the problems we have right now, some NEW thing will come along, and then we'll have to deal with THAT.

I've read that's what happened with the DINOSAURS. They were riding high for a couple hundred million years, and then an asteroid came and wiped them out.

What's really crazy is that cockroaches were around back then, and somehow THEY survived. And they'll probably be here long after we're gone, too. Personally, I think cockroaches are disgusting. But they must be doing SOMETHING right.

SMACK

Speaking of SURVIVAL, right now, I'm just trying to get through middle school. And the last few days haven't been all that great.

Even though it's warm outside, the thermostat at school still thinks it's WINTER. So the furnace is on full blast all day, which makes it hard to concentrate in class.

And it's worse in the CAFETERIA, because there aren't any windows you can open to get fresh air.

The heat has been frying my brain, and I've been forgetting when my school assignments are due. I forgot a really BIG one today, which was my country project for the International Showcase.

Back in November, everyone had to choose a country to do a report on. I picked Italy, because I'm a HUGE pizza fan.

But it turns out Italy was a really popular choice, so my Social Studies teacher had to do a random drawing to decide who got it. And she chose Dennis Tracton, which isn't fair because he's lactose intolerant and can't even eat cheese.

So the teacher assigned me Malta, which I didn't even know was a country.

Anyway, that was two months back, and I didn't give my country project a second thought until TODAY. And the only reason I remembered was because when I got to school, everybody was wearing weird clothes.

I probably should've realized it was International Showcase day when my friend Rowley came by to get me for school wearing a crazy getup. But he's ALWAYS doing strange stuff, so I barely even noticed.

In homeroom, I took a look at Rowley's project to see how much work was involved, and that's when I started to panic.

His report looked like it took a TON of time, and it was pretty obvious his parents helped him with it. Of course Rowley had actually BEEN to the country he got assigned, so I'm sure that made it a lot EASIER for him.

I asked Rowley to be a pal and switch countries with me, but he's kind of selfish, so he wouldn't go for it. That meant I was on my own, and I only had a few hours to do my whole project from SCRATCH. And I didn't know WHERE I was gonna find a tri-fold this late in the game.

That's when I remembered that I had a tri-fold in my LOCKER. I had started my country project the day after it was assigned so I could get ahead of things for once. But when I pulled it out to see how FAR I'd gotten, I was pretty disappointed.

	MYSTERIOUS **MAL**	

This project was 50% of my Social Studies grade, so I was desperate. I tried getting help from my CLASSMATES, but all THAT did was remind me I need to get some smarter friends.

ANY OF YOU GUYS KNOW WHERE MALTA IS?

IN YOUR BUTT!

HAR HAR HAR!

I stayed indoors for recess to work on my project. I didn't have time to go down to the library for research, so I had to do a lot of GUESSING. The only thing I felt pretty sure about was that Malta was near Russia, but I was shaky on everything ELSE.

Once I finished filling out my tri-fold, I started working on the OTHER stuff.

We were supposed to wear our country's "traditional dress" for the International Showcase, so on the way to lunch I picked out some clothes from the Lost and Found in front of the principal's office.

Luckily, there were a few decent items in the box, and I put together an outfit that looked pretty convincing.

Everyone was supposed to bring in a traditional MEAL, too. At lunch, I bought as many items as I could afford, and threw something together that seemed like it might've come from another country.

MEAT LOAF

HOT DOG

ASPARAGUS

The International Showcase was during the last period, and when I set up my project in the gym, I was actually feeling pretty good about things. But I wish I'd gotten assigned a country where they wore lighter clothes, because the furnace was still on full blast.

The heat was getting to some OTHER kids, too, and tempers were starting to flare. At one point, Brazil and Bulgaria got in a fight over table space, and a teacher had to come break it up.

Kids came in from the elementary school to check out our projects and ask questions. But all I had to do to get them to move along was to pretend I only spoke Maltese.

After that, the PARENTS started to arrive. Luckily, MINE couldn't come, because Dad was at work and Mom was at her college. But some kid in my grade has a mom and dad who are actually FROM Malta, which was really bad luck for ME.

I thought they were gonna report me to my teacher, and I was ready to make a run for it. But then something happened that got me off the hook.

The fight that started between Brazil and Bulgaria flared back up and spilled over to the "C" and "D" countries. And before long, the whole GYM was at war.

Luckily the bell rang, and school got dismissed before anyone got seriously hurt. But the whole situation doesn't exactly give me a lot of hope for world peace.

Tuesday

Well, I THOUGHT I was in the clear, but I was wrong. My Social Studies teacher sent a note home to my parents that said I have to do my International Showcase project AGAIN.

So Mom said I can't watch TV or play video games until I finish. I figure I can probably get this thing done by Saturday, but it won't matter anyway. That's because Mom is making me and my brothers have "Screen-Free Weekends."

Mom thinks us kids are addicted to electronics, and they're the reason we misbehave. So she started this new policy where we're not allowed to use any electronics on Saturdays and Sundays, and we have to find other ways to entertain ourselves.

What really stinks is that when Mom catches us BEHAVING on the weekends, she thinks it's PROOF that Screen-Free Weekends are working.

So lately, me and Rodrick have been remembering to MISBEHAVE on Saturdays and Sundays so Mom doesn't think her no-electronics policy is working. And MANNY joins in, too, because I guess he likes to do whatever his big brothers are doing.

Mom says kids these days don't know how to interact with one another, because we're always staring at our screens. So she's been working with me and Rodrick on our "social skills."

One thing Mom's always trying to get me to do is to look her in the eye when I'm talking to her. I can do that for a LITTLE while, but after a few seconds it just gets too weird.

The latest thing Mom's been making me do is practice shaking hands with Dad. But that's awkward for BOTH of us.

Mom wants me to "branch out" and make more friends in the neighborhood. But I'm already friends with ROWLEY, and he's all I can really handle right now.

Even though there are a ton of kids on my street, I really can't see being friends with any of them. I ALREADY feel like I'm making an exception for Rowley, and the options go downhill from there.

Our house is halfway up Surrey Street, and Rowley's house is near the top. Sometimes it's a pain to even go see HIM, because I have to pass by FREGLEY'S house to do it. And nine times out of ten, Fregley is hanging out in his front yard.

Across the street from Fregley is Jacob Hoff, but he almost never comes outside because his parents are always making him practice the clarinet. And on either side of Jacob are Ernesto Gutierrez and Gabriel Johns, who are in my grade.

Ernesto and Gabriel are nice kids and all, but they BOTH have bad breath, so those two are perfect for each other.

Two doors down from me is David Marsh, who's really into karate. He's best friends with Joseph O'Rourke, who's always doing something to get himself injured.

BOUNCE

Next door to Joseph is Mitchell Pickett, who makes a killing selling premade snowballs in the winter. And mark my words, one day that kid's gonna be a MILLIONAIRE.

Mitchell lives next to a boy one year younger than me who everybody calls Speed Bump. But people steer clear of him because his two older brothers are already in jail.

There's a kid named Pervis Gentry who has a tree house in his backyard, and he spends his summers solving neighborhood crimes. But most of the time the person responsible is Speed Bump.

There's a duplex three-quarters of the way down the hill, and the two families who live in it HATE each other.

I can never keep the kids in that house straight, but I know one of them is named Gino because he has a tattoo on his arm, even though he's only something like seven years old.

There's a boy who lives with his grandmother a few doors down, and his name is Gibson.

Everyone calls him Baby Gibson, because no matter how much time goes by he never seems to get any OLDER. For all I know, Baby Gibson is thirty-two years old and he's got kids of his OWN.

There's a playgroup of preschoolers that gets together twice a week at Mrs. Jimenez's house. I don't know which kids are HERS and which ones are her FRIENDS'. What I DO know is that those kids are totally out of control, and the moms don't really seem to care.

There are some older kids on our street, too. Anthony Denard is a sophomore in high school, and he just started shaving. But he got carried away with the razor blade and accidentally shaved off one of his eyebrows.

Anthony drew it back on with a brown marker, but he didn't do a good job, and now one half of his face always looks surprised.

Anthony's best friend is Sheldon Reyes, who tried to make money plowing the neighbors' driveways the first time it snowed this winter.

But Sheldon doesn't have his license yet, and he did a lot of damage in our neighborhood before his dad found out his son was using his truck.

A few doors down from me are the Garza twins, Jeremy and Jameson, who made up their own language when they were toddlers. And when those two are together, no one can understand a word they say.

There are a bunch of GIRLS on my street, too, but they're just as bad as the GUYS.

The Marlee sisters live across from Rowley's house, and all five of them were born within a few years of each other. I don't know what their deal is, but those girls will just randomly attack people who come into their yard.

Emilia Greenwall lives a few doors down from the Marlee sisters. Emilia always dresses like a princess, and I think she's seen too many Disney movies.

Latricia Hooks lives in the one-story house across from the duplex, and she's a six-foot-two high school junior. Rodrick won't go anywhere NEAR Latricia, because she used to bully him when he was MY age.

Latricia's sister Victoria is in love with Ernesto Gutierrez for some reason, and Victoria's best friend, Evelyn Trimble, dresses like a vampire.

In fact, I'm pretty sure Evelyn thinks she IS a vampire, which is one reason I'm glad I don't ride the bus anymore.

I haven't even mentioned HALF the kids who live on my hill. But if I went down the whole list, it'd take FOREVER.

Mom always asks me why I'm not friends with any kids at the BOTTOM of the hill, even though I've told her a million times why that'll never HAPPEN.

Surrey Street is divided into two halves. There's UPPER Surrey Street, which is the hill, and LOWER Surrey Street, which is the flat part at the bottom.

And even though we all live on the same street, the hill kids and the non-hill kids can't STAND one another.

Living on the hill is no fun. First of all, it's really far from the school, and that last stretch at the end of the day is no joke. ESPECIALLY when it's hot like it has been lately.

The worst thing about living on a hill is that there's not a lot you can DO on it. And if you want to play with a ball, you can forget about it.

BONK

BOUNCE BOUNCE

But the kids who live at the BOTTOM of the hill have it MADE. Their part of the street is FLAT, so they can do anything they want down there. That's why all the athletes come from LOWER Surrey Street.

The thing is, the kids who live at the bottom of our street think they OWN it. And if any of us hill people come down there to PLAY, the Lower Surrey Street kids won't LET us.

In fact, the reason it took me four years to learn to ride a bike was because I had to do it in five-second spurts.

But when it SNOWS, the tables are turned. All of a sudden the Lower Surrey Street kids want to use our hill for SLEDDING, but that's when we give those guys a taste of their own medicine.

Most of the time we can keep the Lower Surrey Street kids off the hill. But they're SNEAKY, and sometimes they slip past us.

Last winter, a bunch of the Lower Surrey Street kids bought the same winter gear as the hill kids, and it was WEEKS before any of us caught on.

If you live on Surrey Street, you're either a HILL kid or a NON-hill kid, and there's no switching sides.

There's a kid named Trevor Nix who lived on the hill until last summer, which is when his family moved to a bigger house at the bottom of the street.

But the kids down there still consider Trevor a HILL person, so they won't let him play on the street. Us hill kids think of him as a traitor for moving, and we won't let him sled in the winter. So now Trevor is basically stuck indoors year-round.

There's a lot of bad blood between the Upper Surrey Street kids and the Lower Surrey Street kids, which is why we can't be friends. But whenever I try to explain the situation to Mom, she just doesn't get it.

In fact, NONE of the moms on our street do. They're all friends with each other, and they have no CLUE about what's REALLY going on.

Lately, though, things have been pretty calm on our street. Us hill kids keep to OUR side, and the other guys keep to THEIRS. But if someone does something stupid, this whole place is gonna BLOW.

<u>Sunday</u>

The temperature dropped about fifteen degrees over the weekend, so today my family was out looking for our pet pig.

For Christmas vacation, my family went away and we left the pig in a kennel. But I guess the pig thought it should've come WITH us, and it wasn't too happy about being left behind.

When we got back HOME, the pig let us know
how it felt about not being included on our family
vacation.

After a few days of the pig acting out, Dad
decided enough was enough, and he sent it to
"obedience school." But the next morning we got
a call from the lady who runs the place, and she
said our pig ESCAPED.

We've been putting up signs asking for help finding our lost pig ever since. But that thing is SMART, so I don't think it's LOST. It just doesn't want to be FOUND.

I figure the pig is probably off HIBERNATING somewhere. Mom says pigs don't do that, but if you ask me, I think they SHOULD.

If I was an animal, that's EXACTLY what I'D be doing right now. On the last day of the fall, I think everyone should get in their pajamas and check out until the spring.

When I was younger, I actually TRIED to hibernate, but it didn't work.

I used to get SUPER excited for Christmas, and once December rolled around it was really hard for me to wait until the big day.

So one year on December 1st, I told my parents I was gonna go to sleep, and that they shouldn't wake me up until Christmas morning. I was pretty surprised when they didn't put up a fight.

I went to bed that night, but I only slept until 1:30 p.m. the next day. Then my sleep schedule was screwed up for the next two weeks.

Mom says it's IMPOSSIBLE for human beings to hibernate, but I'm not 100% convinced that's TRUE.

There's this group of wild kids who live in the woods, and everyone calls them the Mingos. You never see the Mingos in the WINTER, and when they make their first appearance in the SPRING, they look like they just woke up.

So if they're not HIBERNATING, I don't know WHAT they're doing all winter.

The rest of us NORMAL people have to grind it out and deal with the cold weather.

And the only way to do THAT is to stay inside as much as possible and keep warm.

When we got back from our trip a few weeks ago, there was a package on our front step. It was a Christmas gift from Aunt Dorothy, and when we opened it, there was a giant BLANKET inside.

That thing was AMAZING. It was really soft, but it was also HEAVY, which is exactly how I like my blankets. The only problem was that the gift was for all three of us boys, and we started fighting over it right away.

We wanted to use the blanket at the same time, so Mom told us we were gonna have to take TURNS with it.

But the three of us have never been any good at SHARING, so Mom had to make a blanket schedule that spelled out who got to use it when.

Blanket Schedule		
6:00 P.M.	7:30 P.M.	9:00 P.M.
Manny	Manny	Manny
6:30 P.M.	8:00 P.M.	9:30 P.M.
Greg	Greg	Greg
7:00 P.M.	8:30 P.M.	10:00 P.M.
Rodrick	Rodrick	Rodrick

But that wasn't really FAIR. Manny has his OWN blanket, so he was double-dipping.

When it was MY turn to use the blanket, I tried to make the most of it.

But it was really hard to enjoy myself, because
Rodrick would start hovering over me when I still
had fifteen minutes left on my shift.

We each got three half-hour shifts a night, but
Rodrick would cheat Manny out of HIS turn by
taking the blanket into the bathroom right before
Manny's shift was supposed to START. Then
Rodrick would sit in there for an HOUR, which
cut into MY shift.

So Mom made a rule that we can't take the blanket into the bathroom.

One night I slept with the blanket in my room, and Rodrick complained because he wanted to use it while he ate breakfast. Mom made a NEW rule that said if you slept with the blanket, it had to be returned downstairs by 8:00 a.m.

By the end of the first week, there were so many rules that Mom had to put them all in a MANUAL, which ended up being something like twenty-five pages long.

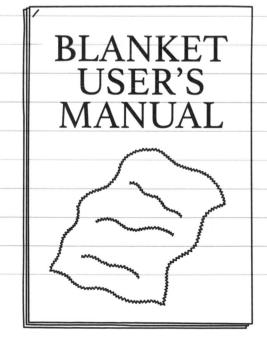

BLANKET USER'S MANUAL

But THAT didn't solve our problems, and eventually Mom took the blanket away to give it to someone who "deserved" it. She said it was our fault we couldn't have something nice, because we didn't know how to SHARE.

Grown-ups are always talking about how great sharing is, but personally, I think it's overrated. And if I ever get enough money, I'm gonna build a big castle all for myself, and there's gonna be a big heavy blanket in every room.

Monday
When I woke up this morning, it was below
freezing outside. I was relieved it actually felt like
WINTER again, but when Mom told me I had to
wear thermal underwear to school, I thought maybe
global warming isn't such a bad thing after all.

I HATE wearing thermal underwear, because it's
uncomfortable, and I feel RIDICULOUS wearing
it. Thermal underwear looks cool when it's on the
mannequin at the mall, but when I put it on, I
just look like a retired superhero.

THERMAL GEAR

The mannequins at the mall are always super buff,
and they make guys like me who can't spend three
hours in the gym every day look bad.

If I ever get in really good shape, I'm gonna sign up to be a mannequin model. Because that would be an awesome thing to brag about on a date.

The mannequins you see at the sports store are always in athletic poses, and it looks like it would be HARD to stay in that position while someone sculpts you. And that's just too much effort for a job that should be EASY.

So when I apply for the job, I'm gonna do it at the bed and bath store.

Mom says I'm LUCKY to have thermal underwear, because our ANCESTORS didn't have this kind of stuff to keep them warm.

Sometimes I WONDER about my ancestors, though. I have no idea why they chose to live HERE when they could've picked somewhere a whole lot WARMER.

But I can't complain, because they SURVIVED, and everything they did led directly to ME. I just wish they could see how I turned out so they'd know all their sacrifices were WORTH it.

I guess we're ALL lucky to be here, because human beings have had to go through a LOT to get to where we are now.

At school, we learned that 10,000 years ago a big sheet of ice covered half the planet. And if people made it through THAT, I guess we can get through ANYTHING.

My teacher said that one day the Earth is gonna be in another ice age and the glaciers will come back, but I hope it doesn't happen anytime SOON.

I've heard glaciers move SLOWLY, which is a good thing. Because maybe we'll have a chance to DO something about it.

I don't know which is worse, a planet that's too HOT or one that's too COLD. All I know is that today it was cold, and it wasn't fun walking to school in the morning.

I tried to cheer myself up by thinking of things I LIKE about the winter, but I came up with a really short list. Christmas is great and all, but after that it's just a long slog to the spring.

I've decided the only thing that actually makes winter worth it is the HOT CHOCOLATE. I used to be on the Safety Patrols, and I'd get free hot chocolate at school. But after I got kicked off, I had to start bringing my OWN.

Lately, I've been filling a thermos with hot chocolate every morning, and that keeps me warm on the walk to school.

But today, Dad must've grabbed MY thermos and left me with HIS. And I didn't realize what had happened until I took a giant gulp of cream of mushroom soup.

I wish Mom and Dad would drive me to school in the morning, but they leave a half hour before I do.

There are some kids on my hill whose parents drive them in on cold days like today. But when me and Rowley try to flag them down to hitch a ride, they won't even make eye contact. And that really stinks, because us hill kids are supposed to have each other's BACKS.

It was so cold out today, the teachers decided to keep us indoors for recess, which was perfectly fine with ME.

The LAST time we had outdoor recess on a day like today, Albert Sandy was saying it was so cold that your spit would freeze before it hit the GROUND.

Well, it turns out he was WRONG, and recess that day was a total NIGHTMARE.

Usually, indoor recess isn't very fun. We're supposed to play board games and do arts and crafts, but kids always get restless and find ways to liven things up.

So today, our teacher said we were gonna try something NEW.

She taught us how to play a game called "Museum," where everyone has to freeze like a statue and hold still for as long as possible.

It was actually pretty FUN, but when recess ended, I realized it was just an easy way to get us to BEHAVE for a half hour.

The thing I don't like about being indoors at school in the winter is that a lot of kids are SICK, and I really don't want someone getting ME sick.

Our school is FULL of germs, and NOBODY covers their mouth when they cough or sneeze.

Walking down the hallway between classes is like walking through a war zone.

Nobody remembers to sneeze into the crook of their arm, and kids like Albert Sandy aren't HELPING things. Today at lunch, Albert told a story about a guy who covered his sneeze, and when he did, he blew his head clean OFF.

I told Albert his story wasn't true, but he swore
it WAS. He said the guy actually SURVIVED,
and now he works as a grocery bagger at the local
Shop-n-Dash.

Albert's ALWAYS spreading bad information like
that, and the kids at my table believe every word
he says. So now there's ZERO chance any of
these guys will cover their mouths the next time
they have to sneeze.

A couple of weeks ago, Albert said that when
someone's pet dies in the winter, they have to wait
until the ground thaws in the spring before it can
be buried. He said they need somewhere to KEEP
their pets in the meantime.

Albert said the people in our town use the school cafeteria's walk-in freezer to store their pets for the winter, and that right now it's full to CAPACITY.

I'm almost POSITIVE this is just another one of Albert's stupid made-up stories. But until we find our PIG, I'm not gonna order the Pork Barbecue Special, just in case.

I'm seriously thinking of changing lunch tables, because I'm tired of sitting with Albert Sandy and all these other idiots every day. One kid I won't miss is Teddy Silvetti, who wears the same sweater all winter long.

Teddy's sweater has NEVER been cleaned, and there are food stains all over it. Sometimes the kids at my table try to guess what each stain IS, which is what they were doing today.

See, this is the reason girls at my school have pictures of pop singers in their lockers. The guys in my grade just aren't giving them any good OPTIONS.

I can't even IMAGINE how many germs are on Teddy's sweater, which is why I sit at least two seats away from him.

Most of my brain power at school goes to keeping tabs on whose germs are WHERE. And I've already filled up two notebooks this winter.

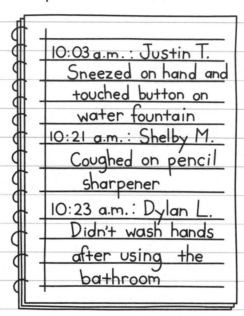

10:03 a.m. : Justin T.
Sneezed on hand and touched button on water fountain
10:21 a.m. : Shelby M.
Coughed on pencil sharpener
10:23 a.m. : Dylan L.
Didn't wash hands after using the bathroom

The times it gets tricky is when you have TWINS like Jeremy and Jameson Garza. I can't tell them apart, and today it looked to me like one was sick, but the other one WASN'T.

COUGH

So I shot a spitball in the sick one's hair to make it easier to keep track of him.

The only GOOD thing about being sick is the cherry lozenges Mom gives me when I have a sore throat. I know you're supposed to suck on them real slow, but I chew those things like CANDY, and I go through a few packs a day.

The girls in my grade LOVE the smell of cherry lozenges, which almost makes being sick WORTH it.

Unfortunately, the GUYS in my grade like the smell, too. And they're always trying to get me to GIVE them some.

A few weeks ago, I thought I felt a sore throat coming on, and I brought three packs of cherry lozenges to school with me. I kept one pack in my pocket and the OTHER two in my locker.

But Jake McGough sniffed out the packs I was keeping in my locker, and by the time I found out, Speed Bump had already picked the lock.

I wish I didn't have to go to school at ALL during cold and flu season. Maybe one day I'll buy one of those big plastic bubbles so I'm not exposed to other kids' germs.

But I'm sure my bubble wouldn't last a DAY before some jerk popped it.

Even though I hate being sick, I'm kind of glad they haven't come up with a cure for the cold yet.

Because if they DID, I wouldn't be able to fake being sick and stay home from school to play video games.

It was even colder today on the walk HOME
than it was on the walk to school. And this time
me and Rowley were facing the WIND, which made
it ten times WORSE.

It was so bad that we had to make a few pit
stops on the way home. The first place we ducked
in was the pizza shop, because there's a big oven
in there, so it's always warm inside. But when the
guy who owns the place realized we weren't gonna
BUY anything, he kicked us out.

Our next stop was the town library. That's a public building, and I knew they couldn't tell us to leave. But when the librarians started getting pushy with the books, we left on our OWN.

I wish we'd used the bathroom in the library before we headed back outside, though, because when we got halfway home, Rowley really needed to go. We knocked on a few doors, but when people saw us, they pretended they weren't home.

We finally got someone to ANSWER, but by that point Rowley's face was so frozen, he couldn't even form WORDS.

By the time we got to Surrey Street, I thought Rowley was gonna have a medical emergency. But I knew none of the Lower Surrey Street people were gonna let us inside their houses.

There's a big ROCK in Mr. Yee's front yard, and I told Rowley he should duck behind it to do his business. Personally, I wouldn't pee outside in THIS kind of cold, because Albert Sandy told us a story about what happened to a guy who DID.

But I didn't feel like it was the right time to mention that to Rowley, and I'm not really sure he had to go number ONE, anyway.

Whatever he was doing back there, he was taking FOREVER. Some of the Lower Surrey Street kids came out of their houses to play, and before long Rowley had drawn a crowd. I just backed off, because I really didn't want people to know I was WITH him.

ZUFF WHUZ
WHUFF WHOO
WHOOO!

Thankfully, Rowley wrapped things up and we got out of there before anyone realized what he was DOING. Because this is just the sort of stupid thing that could end up sparking a WAR.

<u>Tuesday</u>

It was seriously cold again this morning, so I dug my scarf and a pair of old gloves out of the closet. Mom said I should wear the mittens Gramma knitted for me last winter, but when she made those things, she forgot to add the THUMBS.

So whenever I put them on, it's basically like wearing SOCKS on my hands. And they're totally USELESS in a snowball fight.

Mom said I should wear earmuffs, too, but the thing I've learned is that if kids know you can't hear them COMING, you're just ASKING for it.

STEP STEP STEP STEP

The reason I get so cold is because I'm SKINNY, and I don't have any insulation. Every winter, I try to eat a lot to give myself an extra layer of blubber. But I guess I've got a fast metabolism, because nothing I do ever seems to WORK.

CEREAL PLOP ICE CREAM

I think it was something like ten degrees outside this morning, and on the walk to school I started wondering if a person's BLOOD could freeze.

I've heard people are something like 60% WATER, so I guess it's POSSIBLE. But it kind of feels like something Albert Sandy would make up.

What I was worried about the MOST was FROSTBITE. By the time I was halfway to school, my ears were STINGING, and I really wished I had listened to Mom about the earmuffs.

I thought one of my ears might actually fall OFF, and that I wouldn't notice until I was in class.

It wasn't just my EARS I was worried about, though. Apparently there are a LOT of body parts where you can get frostbite.

I wouldn't want to lose my NOSE, because I'd look a little freaky without one. Then again, my desk in Social Studies is right next to the BATHROOM, so at least THAT situation would get a little better.

Plus, my nose ALWAYS runs on cold days, and I never realize I've got frozen snot on my face until it's too late.

I'd like to hang on to my LIPS, too, because if I didn't have them it would always look like I was SMILING. And in certain situations, that could be a real problem.

I was lucky I found those GLOVES, because I wouldn't want to lose any FINGERS, either. The only thing I'd be willing to give up would be my pinky toes, because I hardly EVER use mine. The last time I can remember using them was when I was in preschool and I needed to count to twenty. But other than that, I'm drawing a blank.

I guess a lot of OTHER kids were worried about frostbite, too, because when I got to school, there was a whole line of boys in the bathroom waiting to use the hand dryer. And that made me five minutes late for first period.

It wasn't as windy on the walk home today, but it was just as COLD. Me and Rowley stopped at the pizza place again to warm up, because Rowley found a coupon for two free meatball subs in his coat pocket.

After we left the pizza shop, we still had a long way to walk. But that's when I had an idea.

Gramma's house is halfway between our school and Surrey Street, and I knew there was no one HOME. That's because Gramma goes down south each winter and doesn't come back until the spring.

During the winter, Gramma sends us pictures of herself and her friends in their bathing suits to let us know that she's having a good time.

Gramma takes her dog, Sweetie, with her, too. So while I'm freezing my butt off up here, it's great to know Sweetie is lying on a beach down south soaking up the sun.

Gramma usually keeps a key inside her garden gnome right next to the front door. And sure enough, that's EXACTLY where it was today.

I figured we could use Gramma's house to warm up before the last push home. Rowley was nervous about us going inside with no adults home, but I told him Gramma was FAMILY, and she'd WANT me to use her house while she was away.

When we walked in, I was pretty surprised. It was like an ICEBOX in there, so I guess Gramma turns down the thermostat for the winter.

Usually, Gramma CRANKS the heat. When she's home, it's so warm that you have to eat your ice cream sandwich with the freezer drawer open or the ice cream will melt in your hands.

The first thing I did when we got inside Gramma's was turn up the thermostat. It was taking a while for the house to heat up, though, so I turned on the oven and we warmed up in a HURRY.

Gramma had a bunch of snacks in her refrigerator, and me and Rowley helped ourselves. But while we were eating, we saw some MOVEMENT out the front window.

It was Mrs. McNeil, Gramma's snoopy next-door neighbor. She must've noticed the light from the fridge, and now she was trying to see inside.

We stayed out of sight, and eventually Mrs. McNeil went away. But now I knew we had to be CAREFUL, because I really didn't need her calling the COPS. So we got down low and went into the living room, where Gramma has her TV.

Gramma has ALL the cable channels, and luckily she didn't shut THOSE down for the winter. But we couldn't risk attracting Mrs. McNeil again, so we put a blanket over ourselves AND the television, and watched it THAT way.

I guess we kind of lost track of time, because when we shut off the TV, it was DARK out. By now it was nice and toasty in Gramma's house, and I really didn't wanna go back out there in the cold. So I had an idea for how to make the walk home a little more COMFORTABLE.

I figured if we warmed up our clothes in Gramma's dryer before we headed back out, it would take the edge off for the rest of the trip. So we went down to the basement where Gramma keeps her laundry machines and put in a load of clothes.

We set the timer to thirty minutes and waited.
But it was a little awkward hanging out in our
underwear while the dryer did its thing.

Plus, it was COLD in the basement, so we looked
around for something to WEAR. Rowley found
a sweatshirt I gave Gramma for her birthday,
and he put THAT on. But I didn't feel RIGHT
wearing Gramma's clothes.

I found a sweater that Gramma knitted for
Sweetie, and it fit better than I expected. But
it was a little ITCHY, and I couldn't remember if
Sweetie ever had FLEAS.

But while I was looking around for something to
swap it with, we heard NOISES upstairs.

My FIRST thought was that Gramma gave Mrs.
McNeil a key to the house, and now she was inside.
But Rowley said it might be a BURGLAR who
knew no one was home, and I thought maybe he
was RIGHT.

We heard some more stomping around upstairs, and when the door to the basement opened, we both freaked out.

I looked around for something to use to DEFEND myself, but the best I could come up with was a toilet plunger.

Rowley grabbed a can of lemon dust spray and one of Gramma's purses. And when we heard footsteps coming down the stairs, we braced ourselves.

STOMP
STOMP

WORLD'S BEST GRANDMA

The footsteps PAUSED when they got near the bottom, and that's when we made our MOVE.

It turned out it wasn't Mrs. McNeil, and it wasn't a BURGLAR, either. It was MOM.

She was there to do a load of laundry, since our washing machine at home is broken.

Mom didn't say much. She just told us to get our winter clothes back on and to get in the car. And she was totally silent on the ride back to our neighborhood, which was really AWKWARD.

I figured as soon as Rowley was out of the car, Mom was gonna yell at me for being at Gramma's house without permission. But she didn't say ANYTHING, and she didn't mention it to Dad during dinner, either.

After I finished doing the dishes, Mom told me she wanted to have a talk in my room. She said it was "perfectly normal" for boys my age to play "make believe," and that there was nothing to feel ashamed of. Then she said she was glad me and Rowley were using our imaginations instead of playing video games.

I have no IDEA what Mom thought we were doing in Gramma's basement. But to be honest with you, I kind of wish she had just GROUNDED me instead.

Wednesday

It's been snowing for the past few days, and last night we got another inch and a half. Unfortunately, that wasn't enough to close school, and even if it snowed MORE than that, I don't think they would've given us the day off.

We only get a certain amount of snow days each year, and if we use them all, then we have to make up for them during summer vacation. And we've already burned through most of our snow days for this winter, even though SOME of them technically weren't used because of SNOW.

In December, the school shut down for three days because of a LICE epidemic.

What happened was that Lily Bodner came to
school with head lice, but I guess she didn't know
it. And it SPREAD when she took pictures with
her friends.

So if we're sitting in a hot classroom in July, I
guess we can all thank Lily for taking selfies.

Sometimes, when it snows in the morning, they'll
give us a HALF day. But I'm not a big fan of
half days, because we still have to walk all that
way just to put in a few hours at school.

What REALLY stinks is when the school looks at
the weather forecast and decides in advance that
the NEXT day is gonna be a half day.

On a half day, the school schedule is the same, but everything takes half the time. That goes for DETENTION, too. And all the bullies in our school know that if they do something bad the day BEFORE a half day, they'll only get half the PUNISHMENT.

Sometimes school gets canceled because it's SUPPOSED to snow, and then it DOESN'T. That's because the school relies on our local TV weatherman for the forecast, and he's wrong at least 50% of the time.

On New Year's Eve, he said it was gonna be "T-shirts and shorts weather" the next day, but then it snowed three inches. And when people saw him at the grocery store, they let him know they weren't happy.

Honestly, I don't see how this guy still has a JOB. But I guess as long as people like my parents tune in every night, he's not going ANYWHERE.

I couldn't find one of my gloves this morning, so I looked for a replacement. I was already running late, so the best I could come up with was a puppet Mom bought to try and get me to eat healthy food when I was younger.

MR. MORSELS LOVES VEGETABLES!

NOM NOM NOM!

I guess Mom thought that if Mr. Morsels liked vegetables, then I would, too. But I used Mr. Morsels to eat MY vegetables, and when I found him today in the closet, he still had stains on his face from the peas I wouldn't touch in the second grade.

NOM NOM NOM!

I know it's kind of ridiculous to wear a puppet as a glove, and I MOSTLY remembered to keep that thing tucked in my coat pocket on the walk to school.

But when Cassie Drench rode by in her mom's car, I TOTALLY forgot Mr. Morsels was still on my hand.

HIIII!

Speaking of GIRLS, there's been a BIG change to the Safety Patrols in the past few weeks.

There used to be a lot of BOYS on the Patrols, but most of them quit or got kicked off before the start of the new year.

The last two boys on the Patrols were Eric
Reynolds and Dougie Finch, who were both
captains. But they had their badges taken away
in the first week of January when they got into
a snowball fight in front of the kindergarten
classroom at the elementary school.

So now the Safety Patrols are 100% GIRLS.
And I'll bet they've been planning a takeover for
a WHILE.

The reason is because the guys at my school can
be real JERKS. And when it snows, they're
REALLY bad.

After a while, I'm sure the girls got SICK of it, and that's why they put themselves in charge.

Now that the girls are in power, they're not messing around. If you throw a single snowball on a school day, the Safety Patrols will report you to the principal, and it'll get you an automatic suspension.

So the girls are just PRAYING one of us guys will step out of line.

Today the road was cleared, but the sidewalk WASN'T. Whenever that happens, me and Rowley just walk in the road. But these new Safety Patrols are sticklers for the rules, and they won't let us walk in the street, even though THEY do it.

But it's practically IMPOSSIBLE to walk on the sidewalk when it hasn't been plowed, ESPECIALLY when people are clearing their driveways.

In fact, it's hard to even know where the sidewalk IS, and this morning I almost busted a kneecap on a fire hydrant that was buried in a snowdrift.

The thing that REALLY stinks is that the Safety Patrols make all us guys walk on the SIDEWALK, but they let all the GIRLS walk on the ROAD.

When me and Rowley got to school today, we were totally wiped out from the trip in. But the girls in our class were fresh and ready to go. And if one of them goes on to be president, it's because they got an unfair advantage back in middle school.

I don't really blame the Safety Patrols for sticking it to the guys in my grade. Most boys are basically SAVAGES, and they make civilized guys like ME look bad.

But with this new Safety Patrol situation, I've been thinking there might be a way for me to separate myself from those fools.

If I can work FOR the Safety Patrols, I can stay on their GOOD side. And if I report the troublemakers to the girls, then they'll OWE me.

For some reason, though, snitching is really frowned on in my school. If you tell on a kid for doing something WRONG, then everyone says you're a tattletale, and it's hard to recover from that.

But from what I can tell, the only people the "no snitching" thing helps are the BULLIES. I'm sure they're the ones who came up with the idea in the FIRST place.

Personally, I don't have ANY problem with snitching. And apparently, you can make MONEY off of being a tattletale.

Rodrick told me about a guy in his high school who turned out to be a "narc," which means the guy PRETENDED to be a high-schooler, but he was actually a cop in DISGUISE.

I've heard about this kind of thing before, and sometimes I wonder if there are narcs in MIDDLE school, too.

There's a new kid named Shane Browning who came to our school in the middle of the year, and he looks a lot older than the rest of us. I'm starting to wonder if maybe HE'S a narc.

So I've been giving him the inside scoop on my classmates, just in case he is.

Anyway, the snow situation is causing a LOT of problems. For the past few days, kids have been wearing their boots in school, and everyone tracks snow through the hallways.

So today, the teachers made everyone take off their boots in the entryway. But the snow on the boots MELTED and made a giant PUDDLE.

Then kids WALKED through the puddle on their way to class, and before long everyone's socks were SOAKED. One thing led to another, and by third period it was just complete CHAOS in the hallways.

It got so bad the teachers had to collect all of our socks and keep them in the front office.

But a bunch of barefoot middle schoolers isn't such a great thing, either.

At the end of the day, we all went to the front office to get our socks. But most socks look the SAME, so no one could tell which ones belonged to who.

Luckily, Jake McGough has a really good sense of smell, and he paired each kid up with their correct socks.

He even got the socks right for the Garza twins,
which you have to admit is pretty IMPRESSIVE.

I was glad it was a little warmer on the way home
today, since me and Rowley didn't have Gramma's
house to use as a pit stop. But that didn't mean
the walk home was EASY.

You're not allowed to throw snowballs on the way
home from school. But AFTER you get home, you
can do anything you WANT.

So kids who live close to school have figured out that
if they drop their bags off at their houses, that
counts as being HOME. Then they come after the
kids like me and Rowley who still have a long way to
WALK.

The SAFETY PATROLS get ambushed, too.
But rules are rules, and they're not allowed to
fight BACK.

And they get attacked from both SIDES. Some
of the kids on my hill who get rides home walk
halfway back to school just to get their licks in.

It's supposed to snow another few inches tomorrow. I told my parents that I'm saving up for a SNOWMOBILE so getting to school isn't such a hassle on days like today.

But Mom and Dad started listing all the reasons why a middle school kid can't have a snowmobile, and after a while I kind of tuned them out.

Any time I come up with a good idea, my parents shoot it down. They did the same exact thing when I had my dogsled idea LAST winter.

I figured if I bought a few dogs and trained them to pull a sled, getting to school in the morning would be a SNAP.

I guess my parents thought I was JOKING, though, because they told me I should go for it.

But when I used my Christmas money to buy a litter of puppies from the lady up the street, Mom and Dad made me return every last one.

<u>Thursday</u>
Today reminded me why the winter is my least
favorite time of year.

It was another snowy day, but this morning I
decided to do some extra preparation to stay warm
on the way to school. Dad lit a fire before he left
for work, and I figured I could use it to warm
up my coat and boots before I put them on.

But I put my boots too close to the fire, and
the rubber soles melted into the bricks. So when it
was time to go, they wouldn't BUDGE.

Rowley was coming by to get me at any minute, so
I had to figure out something ELSE to wear on
my feet.

I knew the Safety Patrols wouldn't let us walk in the street, and my sneakers were gonna get SOAKED if I had to walk through the snow.

So I created my own SNOWSHOES out of pizza boxes and duct tape. And by the time Rowley knocked on the door, I was ready to go.

I've gotta say, my snowshoes worked even better than I EXPECTED. In fact, I was moving along so fast that Rowley had trouble keeping up with me.

SKISH

SKOOSH

But once we got to the bottom of Surrey Street, things fell apart.

The boxes got SOGGY, and I started sinking into the snow. And then it was even WORSE than having sneakers on, because now I was dragging these wet BOXES along with me.

SPLURK   SPLURK

I knew this wasn't working, so I had Rowley try to help me pull the boxes off my sneakers. But it was practically IMPOSSIBLE, because they were double-wrapped in duct tape.

CHEW   GNAW

Unfortunately, we were right at the edge of the Guzmans' yard, and they've got about eleven dogs. The dogs were curious about what we were doing, and that wasn't helping things.

Then the dogs got AGGRESSIVE and started fighting over the pizza boxes. That's when I remembered there were a few slices of pizza still in them.

The dogs chewed up the pizza boxes, and thankfully didn't take off my FEET. We got out of there as quick as we could, but my sneakers were getting soaked in the snow.

The second I stepped onto the street, though, the Safety Patrols were right there with their whistles. So I had to just suck it up and walk on the sidewalk.

It didn't take long for the COLD to set in. I was worried I could lose my TOES if I didn't find a way to warm them up. But the school was still a long way off, and I was desperate.

So we stopped every few houses, and I'd shove my feet into a dryer vent until I got the feeling back in my toes.

We finally made it to school. But it took me a minute to realize it was almost as cold in THERE as it was OUTSIDE.

Apparently what happened was that the sock smell from yesterday was so strong that it was too much for the night janitor.

So he went around and opened all the windows to let some fresh air circulate.

But then he forgot to CLOSE the windows at the end of his shift. And the furnace couldn't keep up, so it shut down. That meant we had a whole day of school with NO HEAT.

At first the teachers let us wear our winter stuff in class. But I guess that was too weird, so they changed their minds and made us put our gear in the lockers.

In History we were FREEZING, but our teacher was just FINE. Mrs. Willey keeps a space heater next to her desk, and she had that thing cranked up to the MAX.

Halfway through class, a girl named Becky Cosgrove tipped over her desk and started yelling, which was totally random.

As punishment, Mrs. Willey made Becky sit in a chair next to her desk. And it took a minute for the REST of us to figure out what Becky's game was.

But kids in middle school are idiots, and within thirty seconds EVERYONE was trying to get a seat next to Mrs. Willey.

For the rest of the day, everybody did whatever they could to keep WARM. And some kids got pretty CREATIVE about it.

We had a school play a few weeks ago, and somebody had the bright idea to get one of the costumes from behind the stage.

While most of us were freezing our butts off INSIDE, the snow was really piling up OUTSIDE. And by fourth period, people were freaking out that we were gonna be stuck at school OVERNIGHT.

At lunch, kids bought up everything in the cafeteria so they'd have something to eat if we got snowed in. That sent everyone ELSE into a panic, so kids made a run on the vending machines in the hallways.

SHAKE
SHAKE

At that point, people were just trying to get their hands on anything that was EDIBLE. A rumor spread that there was food in the SCIENCE lab, so a bunch of kids ran down THERE.

And from what I heard, they picked that place CLEAN.

I think the principal could see that she was about to have a RIOT on her hands, so she announced an early dismissal.

Well that was great news for everyone who rode the BUS home, but us kids who had to WALK didn't have it so easy. I really wasn't looking forward to walking home in a snowstorm, so I came up with an IDEA. Whirley Street isn't too far from OUR neighborhood, so I figured me and Rowley could ride on THEIR bus and then WALK the rest of the way.

So after we got dismissed, we headed straight for the bus line. And we were so bundled up, nobody even NOTICED when we got on board.

I've gotta say, it was kind of WEIRD being on the bus with the Whirley Street kids, because those guys are our ENEMIES. They used to sled on our hill every winter until they discovered the 13th hole at the golf course.

The 13th hole is LEGENDARY, and everyone knows it's the best sledding hill in our town. But the problem is that the golf course is part of the country club, so if you sled there, you're TRESPASSING.

Last year I wanted to see what the fuss over the 13th hole was all about, so I got Rowley to come with me. But Rowley was SUPER nervous about the trespassing thing, so he didn't want to go.

I had to remind Rowley that he and his family are MEMBERS of the country club, so technically he WOULDN'T be trespassing.

But I guess Rowley was worried his family might lose their membership if he got caught sledding. So to disguise himself, he shook his face really fast, and kept that up the whole time we were there.

SHAKE
SHAKE

I've gotta admit, the 13th hole was everything people SAID it was.

118

It was really STEEP, and someone built up a mound of snow near the bottom where kids were catching some SERIOUS air.

We got in a few good runs, but that's when the WHIRLEY Street kids came and kicked everyone ELSE off the golf course so they could have it to THEMSELVES.

But I was OK with it. As long as those guys aren't causing trouble on OUR street, they can have the whole GOLF COURSE for all I care.

The bus ride with the Whirley Street kids wasn't a lot of fun, but me and Rowley just tried to keep a low profile so no one would notice us.

We were almost to Whirley Street when one of the kids in the back did something really DUMB. Some fool actually threw a snowball ON THE BUS.

ZIP

SPLAT

The second it happened, the driver pulled over. She said she wasn't moving until the person who threw the snowball turned themself in.

Like I said before, there's a "no snitching" rule in middle school, so no one from the back of the bus made a PEEP. I wish I knew who did it, because I would've given them up in a HEARTBEAT.

I was pretty sure the bus driver was just BLUFFING about not moving, and that we'd be on our way within a few minutes.

But then she broke out a BOOK, and started on page ONE. So we just sat there and waited for an HOUR while she read.

The worst part about the whole thing was that the bus driver turned off the ENGINE, so there was no HEAT.

There was some conversation going on in the back of the bus, and I think a few kids were trying to get the one who threw the snowball to give himself up.

But I really wish I hadn't turned around to look, because when I DID, some eighth grader realized I wasn't from Whirley Street.

That was all it took. These guys needed someone to take the BLAME for the snowball, and since I was an OUTSIDER, it was a no-brainer for them.

The bus driver said I needed to get off the bus IMMEDIATELY. That was fine with ME, because now that my cover was blown, I didn't wanna stick around any longer than I HAD to. So I got off the bus, and Rowley was two steps behind me.

VROOM

I was pretty sure we were about a mile from
Surrey Street. The road we were on didn't have
sidewalks, but there weren't any Safety Patrols
this far out, so we walked on the street.

Five minutes later, we heard angry voices. It was
a bunch of Whirley Street kids, and they were
coming straight FOR us.

First, those idiots LIED about me throwing the
snowball on the bus. Then they BELIEVED their
lie, and now they were MAD.

Me and Rowley had to make a choice. We could
either deal with the mob, or RUN. We decided
to run, and the only place to go was into the
WOODS.

Believe me, that was the LAST thing I wanted to do. Everyone knows the woods along that road are where the GOAT MAN lives, which is why nobody ever goes in there.

Rodrick was the first one to tell me about the Goat Man, who he said was a half man, half goat.

I wasn't sure if he meant the top half was a GOAT and the bottom part was a MAN, or if it was the other way around. But either way, the Goat Man seemed pretty scary to ME.

Me and Rowley have argued for YEARS over which version is right. Rowley thinks the Goat Man is split down the MIDDLE.

I guess Rowley could be RIGHT, but if you ask me, I think his version sounds kind of STUPID.

It's fun talking about this stuff when we're on a sleepover and safe in our sleeping bags. But now that we were in the woods where the Goat Man actually LIVES, it was no laughing matter.

The Whirley Street kids must've known about the Goat Man, too, because when we went into the woods, they didn't follow us. I figured we'd stay in there just long enough for the Whirley Street kids to LEAVE, because we didn't want to be in there any longer than we HAD to.

But those guys must've known we were too chicken to stay in there for long, and we could see them waiting for us on the road at the edge of the woods.

So our only choice was to go deeper in, and that's what we did.

What was WEIRD was how QUIET it was in there. After a while, I realized we couldn't hear the cars on the road, and that's when I knew we went in TOO deep.

We followed our footsteps back to the road, but the sun was going down, and it was getting hard to find our tracks.

We picked up the pace, because we didn't wanna get stuck in the woods in the DARK. But when we came across a set of tracks, we FROZE.

At first we thought it was the GOAT MAN. But then we realized there were TWO sets of footprints, and they were OURS. That meant we'd spent the past ten minutes walking in a giant CIRCLE.

So we turned around and headed in the OTHER direction. But then we ran into a CREEK, and I knew we were lost.

GURGLE GURGLE

Rowley was in a PANIC, but I wasn't. I knew that if you get lost in the wilderness, as long as you have WATER, you're FINE.

I saw a movie where these explorers got trapped in the mountains, but they found a spring and it kept them alive.

But then I remembered that when they got DESPERATE, they had to eat their pack animals. I just hoped things didn't reach that point for US.

I figured if we followed the creek, it might LEAD us somewhere, and at least we wouldn't get lost again. But when we came across a beaver dam, Rowley started freaking out.

Rowley said beavers are DANGEROUS, and that
he saw a show on TV where a beaver attacked a
PERSON.

But Rowley's an idiot. The show he was talking
about was a CARTOON, and I was actually
WITH him when he watched it.

WHAPPITY WHAPPITY WHAP

Still, I couldn't convince Rowley to stay near the
creek, so we had to turn around AGAIN. And by
now it was REALLY dark. After walking a few
more minutes, something bright caught my eye. I
thought maybe it was the headlights from a car,
and we ran toward it.

It turned out the light WAS coming from a car, but it was just a rusted-out piece of junk in the middle of the woods. And what caught my eye was the reflection of the MOON on the bumper.

When my eyes adjusted to the light, I realized there were a LOT of abandoned cars and trucks all around us.

I saw something shiny sitting on a stump and I picked it up. The thing was cold and metal, and when I held it up to my face to take a closer look, I knew EXACTLY what it was.

It was a BELT BUCKLE, and it belonged to MECKLEY MINGO.

That meant me and Rowley were smack in the middle of the Mingos' CAMP.

People in my town have always wondered where the Mingos live, and now me and Rowley had stumbled into their HEADQUARTERS.

I thought we were LUCKY, because at least there was no one THERE. But when I turned to LEAVE, something grabbed my HAND.

Well, technically, something grabbed Mr. Morsels. I thought for SURE it was Meckley Mingo and he was gonna KILL me for touching his belt buckle.

Thankfully, I was WRONG. The puppet was snagged on a truck's door handle, so I tried to pull it free.

That's when we heard noises coming from INSIDE THE TRUCK. I realized I had to choose between saving MYSELF and saving a PUPPET, and it was no contest.

Me and Rowley tore out of there. But when we were a good distance away from the Mingos' camp, we heard a sound that made my blood run cold.

AROOOOOOOOO

I didn't know if it was the GOAT MAN or the MINGO KIDS.

All I knew for sure was that if we stopped RUNNING, we'd be DEAD.

I could hear shouting behind us, and it was getting CLOSER. But just when it felt like the voices were right on TOP of us, we broke through the trees and into the open.

Luckily, Dad was paying ATTENTION, or me and Rowley would've been ROADKILL.

But at least it would've been over QUICK. Because if the MINGOS caught us, I'm sure they would've taken their TIME.

Friday
When I woke up this morning, I was totally
EXHAUSTED. My legs felt like rubber from all
that running yesterday, and I barely got any
rest because I had a nightmare the Mingos were
chasing me.

I was gonna tell Mom I couldn't go to school
today, but when I looked out the window, I
realized I didn't HAVE to.

It snowed at least five inches overnight, which meant school was CLOSED. So I was looking forward to a nice, relaxing day of doing absolutely NOTHING.

Mom and Dad were already gone, and Manny was at daycare. Rodrick usually sleeps past 1:00 p.m. on snow days, so I more or less had the whole house to MYSELF.

I went downstairs to make a bowl of cereal and turn on the TV. But there was something wrong with the REMOTE.

PRESS
PRESS

I noticed it felt a little LIGHT, so I opened up the back of the remote to see if there was a missing battery.

It turns out there weren't ANY batteries inside, but there was a note from MOM.

To get the batteries
for the remote,
load the dishwasher.

I really didn't feel like doing chores on a SNOW DAY, so I looked around the house for some batteries I could put in the remote. But Mom must've KNOWN I'd do that, because there wasn't a spare battery ANYWHERE.

JIGGLE
JIGGLE

I couldn't figure out how Mom was gonna know I loaded the dishwasher, since she wasn't even HOME. But when I put in the last plate and shut the door, I found something.

It was another NOTE with a BATTERY taped to it.

Congratulations!
Clean the downstairs bathroom to get your next battery!

I didn't like where this was heading. The TV remote takes FOUR batteries, and at this rate I was gonna burn through my whole DAY doing chores.

But then I realized I didn't HAVE to. The remote in Mom and Dad's bedroom is really SKINNY, and I was pretty sure it only took ONE battery.

And it turned out I was RIGHT. I knew I was gonna have to finish all the chores before Mom and Dad got home, but I figured I had plenty of time and I deserved to enjoy myself for a little while. So I made myself comfortable on their bed and turned on the TV.

Ordinarily I get a little weirded out being in Mom and Dad's bed, but today I decided to make an exception. ESPECIALLY when I realized one of their blankets was the one we got from Aunt Dorothy for Christmas.

Watching TV in bed was AWESOME, or at least for a WHILE. I was comfortable for the FIRST two hours, but after that my neck started hurting from lying in that position.

I've already decided that when I get a place of my own, I'm gonna attach my TV to the CEILING so I can look straight UP at it. But I'm gonna have someone install the TV who knows what they're DOING, because I don't need to be the next Flat Stanley.

I must've dozed off for a while, because when the phone rang it startled me. It was MOM, and I thought she was checking in on me to see if I'd finished my chores.

But the reason she was calling was to tell me she couldn't make it home in time to pick up Manny at daycare, so she was gonna have Mrs. Drummond drop Manny off at the HOUSE.

That meant I had to BABYSIT, which was gonna really mess up the rest of my day.

When Mrs. Drummond dropped off Manny a half hour later, I didn't know what to DO with him. I put Manny in Mom and Dad's room and turned on some cartoons, but he followed me back downstairs. So I guess Manny just wanted to be with ME.

I tried to remember what Rodrick used to do with me when I was little. But all I could think of was the time he gave me lemon juice and told me it was SODA.

Then I remembered a game me and Rodrick used to play that was actually FUN. We pretended the floor was LAVA, and we had to stay OFF of it by using cushions and pillows from the couch.

Me and Rodrick used to play that game for HOURS. I figured if I got Manny started, he could keep himself entertained while I wrapped up my chores. But when I told Manny how the game WORKED, he totally freaked out.

So now Manny wouldn't go anywhere near the FLOOR. And that made things really inconvenient for me.

But I still had to do my chores, or I'd be in trouble when Mom and Dad got home. And I had a BIG one in front of me, which was shoveling the driveway.

I knew Manny would have a total meltdown if I left him inside with all that lava, so I got him dressed in his snow gear, which wasn't easy.

I figured Manny could play on the back deck while I shoveled the driveway, and he'd be safe because the deck is closed in.

The snow in the driveway was wet and heavy, and it was hard to make any progress. After a half hour, I decided to take a break and soak my hands in some warm water.

While I was inside, I thought I'd check and see how Manny was doing out on the back deck. But Manny was GONE. He had built a little staircase out of snow to escape.

Thankfully, he didn't get FAR. But I realized I couldn't leave him ALONE anymore.

I took Manny to the front yard with me. It was getting late, and Dad gets REALLY mad when the driveway's not cleared when he comes home from work.

So I shoveled as fast as I could, and Manny pitched in to help.

But there was just too much snow, and not enough TIME. I was ready to give up when some girls from a different neighborhood walked by and offered to clear our driveway for ten bucks.

These kids looked YOUNG, and I didn't see how they could do any better than me and Manny. But we could use all the help we could get, so I was willing to give them a CHANCE.

I had five dollars in the drawer next to my bed, and I got the other five from the big jar of change Manny has in his room. But what I didn't realize when I agreed to the deal with those girls was that they had a SNOWBLOWER.

So they were done clearing the whole driveway inside of five minutes.

I felt like I was getting ripped off, so I told them I'd pay them three bucks instead of ten.

But I guess this wasn't the FIRST time someone tried to stiff them on payment. They moved all the snow BACK into the driveway and added the snow from the front lawn just to make a point.

By the time my PARENTS got home, things were worse off than when I STARTED.

After dinner, Mom and Dad lectured me until about eight o'clock for not finishing my chores. And that's when Rodrick got out of bed to start his day.

<u>Saturday</u>
I usually sleep IN on weekends, but this morning Mom had OTHER plans for me.

She said I was going to spend the whole day OUTSIDE. I told her I'd go out in the snow after I played some video games, but she reminded me about Screen-Free Weekends, and I knew she wasn't gonna budge.

When I was younger, I could spend HOURS playing in the snow. But nowadays, after about ten minutes, I'm ready to come inside.

Grown-ups act like being in the snow is the most fun you can ever have. But you never see THEM out there rolling around in it.

I can only remember one time Dad played with us out in the snow. But THAT ended the second Rodrick dumped snow down the back of Dad's NECK.

Mom's ALWAYS making us kids go outside, because she says we need our vitamin D, which you get from the sun. I tell Mom I get PLENTY of vitamin D from the sun in my video games, but that kind of reasoning never works on her.

When I went outside today, Manny was already in the front yard making snowmen, or WHATEVER you'd call those things.

We never finished raking the lawn in the fall, so Manny used the leaves we didn't pick up to decorate his snow friends.

Manny had used up most of the snow in the yard, so there wasn't a whole lot I could even DO outside. I decided to head up to Rowley's, which meant I had to pass by FREGLEY'S house. And sure enough, he was out in his front yard.

The reason I went to Rowley's was because his family just got heated floors. So on cold days, I try to spend as much time at his house as POSSIBLE.

But Mom must've KNOWN I was gonna go to Rowley's, because she called his parents and he was outside when I got there.

As long as we both had to be outdoors, I figured we should make the most of it. Since I'd already done all the hard work of getting up the hill, I told Rowley we should get in a little sledding.

The plow usually comes through by late morning, so we can only get in a few good runs before the street is cleared. But the regular plow guy was on VACATION, and the kids at the top of the hill told the SUBSTITUTE driver that Surrey Street was two miles down the road. So that bought us some extra time.

I don't actually think it's a good idea to mess around with substitutes, because it ALWAYS comes back to bite you. Last year we had a long-term sub in Algebra, and on his first day, me and my classmates all switched seats with each other because we knew the sub would be relying on the seating chart.

ROBERT, DID YOU FINISH YOUR HOMEWORK?

YEP!

ROBERT

HAR HAR HAR!

I've gotta say, it was pretty hilarious having him call us by the wrong names every day. But when the kid pretending to be ME started acting like a total JERK, it wasn't so funny anymore.

And when our REAL teacher got back, the sub gave her a write-up on the FAKE Greg Heffley, which landed ME in detention for two weeks.

Rowley only has one sled, but there's just enough room on it for two people. We squeezed on board and pointed it down the hill, but with all that weight, we couldn't really get any momentum.

SCOOT   SCOOT

When we got close to the bottom of the hill, we came to a dead stop. But that was probably a GOOD thing, because the kids who made it all the way down got nailed by the Lower Surrey Street kids when they crossed into their territory.

SMAP

BAP

PIFF

Things could've gotten a lot uglier, but then the substitute snowplow driver figured out where Surrey Street was, and that was the end of THAT.

I decided we had been outside long enough, and we tried to go inside. But Mom had locked the door, and I could tell she wasn't messing around.

Since we couldn't SLED anymore, we needed to figure out something ELSE to do. So me and Rowley went to the empty lot a few doors up from my house to decide what to do NEXT.

I figured as long as we had to be outside, we might as well stay WARM. At school, we watched a movie about people in the Arctic who build IGLOOS to survive in the cold weather, and I thought maybe we could give it a try.

We made some snow bricks and stacked them the way the people in the movie did. It was hard at first, but then we started getting the HANG of it. The main thing was getting the shape of the dome just right so it didn't COLLAPSE.

We were really careful, and everything held together. But when we put in the last brick at the top, we realized we forgot to build a DOOR.

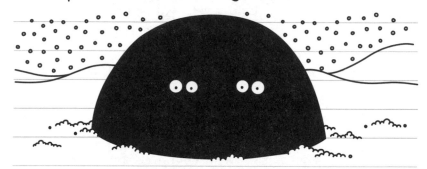

Rowley started hyperventilating, and I knew if I didn't DO something, he was gonna suck up all the oxygen in there. So I busted through the top and took a big gulp of fresh air.

Some neighborhood kids had been watching us build our igloo, and with my head sticking up, I must've looked like an easy target.

After those idiots ran out of snowballs, they climbed on top of the igloo. But it wasn't meant to support any extra weight, and within a few seconds the whole thing came crashing down.

Me and Rowley were lucky to crawl out of there ALIVE. Once we pulled ourselves out of our ruined igloo, I decided that we'd had enough fun for one day. So we went back to the house, and this time Mom let us IN.

I told Mom what happened at the empty lot,
and how she needed to go out there and yell at
those stupid kids for us.

But Mom said that learning to deal with "conflict"
is part of growing up, and that me and Rowley
were gonna have to deal with this on our OWN.
I didn't like the sound of THAT. I thought the
whole POINT of having parents is that you've
got someone to solve your problems FOR you.

Dad was listening from the other room, and he
had a TOTALLY different take. He said that
the neighborhood kids had just declared WAR on
me and Rowley, and if we didn't fight BACK,
they'd think it was OK to attack us whenever
they WANTED.

Dad said that when HE was growing up, his
neighborhood turned into a BATTLEFIELD every
time it snowed. Kids built giant snow forts and
had epic snowball fights, and everyone was part of
a different "clan."

Dad said each clan had its own FLAG, and when
you captured somebody else's fort, you planted a
flag to mark your territory.

Well, Rowley thought WE should form a clan,
and he really liked this FLAG idea. I thought
it seemed kind of DUMB, but as long as making
a flag gave us an excuse to be INDOORS for a
while, I was all for it.

We found an old pillowcase in the laundry room, and got some markers out of the junk drawer in the kitchen. We started by trying to come up with a NAME for our clan.

Rowley said he wanted us to be "Hufflepuff," but I said if we were gonna do this, I wanted our name to be something ORIGINAL.

We argued back and forth for a while about our name, and I realized we weren't gonna agree on one. So we talked about how our flag should LOOK.

Rowley wanted our symbol to be a WOLF, but I wanted something even fiercer than THAT, so we'd scare kids off. I thought a bloody battle-axe would do the trick, but of course Rowley didn't like that idea. So we compromised and put the two things TOGETHER.

But when you add an axe and a wolf, you just get a dead wolf, which isn't gonna scare ANYONE.

We were going to start over and make a new flag, but when I got another pillowcase, Mom told us we needed to go back outside. So we got on our snow gear and went to the empty lot.

The kids who wrecked our igloo had moved on to other things, so me and Rowley had the empty lot all to ourselves. We used the snow from the igloo as a starting point, and made a fort that could hold up to an attack.

After we were finished, we planted our flag on top of the wall and WAITED.

I figured our fort might attract some attention, but I didn't realize just how MUCH. Within a few minutes we had kids coming at us from every DIRECTION.

We were COMPLETELY outgunned, and when the kids rushed our fort, we had to ABANDON it.

BLAP

SPLAT

When we got back to the house, we told Dad what happened. But after we described our fort to him, he said we did everything all WRONG.

He said we needed to build our fort on HIGH ground so we could drive back our enemies.

Then Dad launched into a big history lesson on castle warfare and all the things that people did to defend themselves back in medieval times.

The stuff they did in the old days was totally BRUTAL, and here's just one example. When invaders tried to climb the walls of a castle, the people inside would pour boiling OIL on them.

I hope it doesn't get to that level in our neighborhood battles. But tonight, I added an item to Mom's grocery list just in case it DOES.

Shopping List	
Eggs	Peas
Milk	Pears
Ketchup	Batteries
Bread	OIL
Pickles	

Sunday

It must've snowed another seven inches last night, and the street was totally COVERED when I woke up. I couldn't even see the line between our YARD and the ROAD.

I was kind of surprised the plow hadn't come yet, because when there's THIS much snow, people can't even get their cars out of their driveways. But when Dad came back from his morning walk, I found out what was going on.

Dad said that when the plow tried to get up the hill, it got STUCK. And when the snowplow driver got ambushed by the neighborhood kids, he ran off and left the truck sitting in the street.

SPLAT

BLAP

That meant we could sled all DAY if we wanted to. But sledding is for KIDS, and I had OTHER plans in mind.

I'd been up all night looking through Dad's books to learn everything I could about castle warfare and battle strategies. And by the morning, I was READY.

I wanted to get started making a fort with Rowley right away, but I knew that the second we put up WALLS, we were gonna be under ATTACK. The only way we could fight back was if we had AMMUNITION.

I figured we could buy a big supply of premade snowballs from Mitchell Pickett, so we went down to his shed, which was open for business. But I guess things must've gone well for Mitchell last winter, because THIS year he EXPANDED his operations.

I'd borrowed enough money from Manny's change jar to pay for three dozen snowballs, but now that I saw all this OTHER stuff, I had to make some tough choices.

The Sloppy Specials looked like regular snowballs to me, so I asked Mitchell why they were five times more expensive. He said that each one was a regular snowball with SLUSH on the inside, and don't even ask me how he pulled THAT off.

We ended up buying two dozen premade snowballs and one snowball launcher, which I figured we could use if we needed to nail somebody from long distance.

But I wish I'd brought the whole jar of change, because Mitchell was selling a snow catapult that looked like it could REALLY do some damage.

I'd have to get that another time, though. We loaded up my sled with our purchases and went back to the empty lot.

But when we got closer, we were SHOCKED by what we saw. There were a BUNCH of snow forts in the empty lot now, and there were kids inside each one.

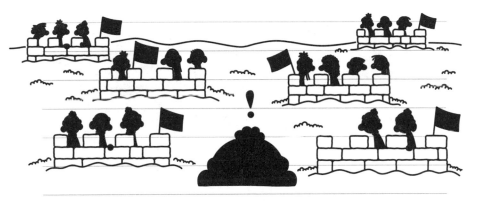

These kids copied our idea, right down to the FLAGS. The Marlee sisters had a spear on their flag, and Evelyn Trimble had a bat on hers. The Garza twins had a two-headed ogre, which actually looked pretty cool.

There were some really LAME flags, too. Marcus Marconi's dad owned the sub shop in the center of town that went out of business, and Marcus used the flag that used to hang in front of the restaurant.

I wanted to get closer to see who ELSE made a fort, but when we got near the empty lot, Ernesto, Gabriel, and a bunch of OTHER kids opened FIRE on us.

The lot was totally overcrowded, and I knew there was no WAY we could build a snow fort there now. So our only chance was to take over someone ELSE'S.

I got some old binoculars from my garage so we could scope things out without having to get too CLOSE.

Things had gotten a lot CRAZIER in the five minutes we were gone, though. Gabriel and Ernesto were in a battle with the Marlee sisters, and a bunch of homeschooled kids were battling with the Garza twins.

Emilia Greenwall and Evelyn Trimble had teamed up to fight Anthony Denard and Sheldon Reyes, and Speed Bump and Latricia Hooks were straight-up going at it with their FISTS.

But I wasn't focused on all that. I was searching for a fort that looked VULNERABLE, and I FOUND one. The duplex kids had built a pretty solid-looking fort, but as usual it looked like they weren't getting along.

I figured they'd wear themselves out fighting, and when they DID, me and Rowley could POUNCE. So we moved in a little closer and waited for the right moment.

That's when I noticed a fort that didn't have anyone IN it. The fort was sitting all alone on top of a big mound of snow. I remembered what Dad said about the HIGH ground, and this fort was in the PERFECT spot.

I couldn't figure out why someone would build a fort and ABANDON it, but I knew this was our big chance. So we snuck around it and climbed over the back wall.

It turned out the fort WASN'T empty, though. It belonged to BABY GIBSON, who was inside with a stockpile of snowballs.

But the second we stepped in the fort, it was under ATTACK.

The homeschooled kids must've known about the high-ground thing, too, and now they wanted the fort for THEMSELVES. But when they came charging up the mound, we drove them back. And even Baby Gibson got in on the act.

Then kids started coming for us from every direction, and it was getting harder and harder to defend the fort.

The duplex kids split into two groups, and they came at us from the left AND the right, while Ernesto and Gabriel started using snowball throwers to snipe at us from THEIR fort.

And while we were trying to deal with all THAT, some little kid from Mrs. Jimenez's playgroup tunneled up through the bottom of our fort and TOTALLY took us off guard.

The next thing we knew, our fort was totally infested with PRESCHOOLERS. And to cap it all off, the Marlee sisters did a sneak attack from the rear, which was terrifying, because those girls go for the EYES.

Me and Rowley got driven out of the fort and onto the open battlefield, where it was just total MAYHEM. Everyone was fighting everyone ELSE, and any sense of order was just GONE.

Then something happened that made everyone STOP. Joe O'Rourke got hit in the mouth with an ice ball and lost a couple of TEETH.

In our neighborhood, ice balls are on the "banned" list in snowball fights. So when somebody crossed that line, everybody knew things had gone too far.

Representatives from all the clans had a meeting in the center of the empty lot to settle on the RULES.

Everyone agreed that ice balls were off-limits, and so was yellow snow. We came up with a bunch of OTHER rules, too, like how it's not OK to stuff snow in someone's hat and then put it back on their head.

Once we agreed on everything, we were ready for the next round of battle.

But while we were doing all that TALKING, we didn't notice what was happening right BEHIND us.

The Lower Surrey Street kids had snuck up to the top of the hill with their sleds, and by then, there was nothing we could do to STOP them.

Now, if there's ONE thing that unites us hill kids, it's when the kids from the BOTTOM of the hill try to take what's OURS. We don't have much, but we have the HILL, and no one's gonna take that from us.

As long as the plow was stuck, we knew those guys were just gonna keep COMING.

So we decided to DO something about it.

The only way to keep the Lower Surrey Street kids from coming back up the hill was to build a WALL to block their path. And we didn't wanna build some puny wall they could just push over, either. We wanted something that was SOLID.

But we needed to make it FAST, because those guys were already marching back up the hill with their sleds. So we got recycling bins from some nearby houses and started BUILDING.

SHPLOP

We made it a DOUBLE wall, so if anyone broke through the first layer, they'd still have to deal with the SECOND one. And we stockpiled a TON of snowballs.

We weren't gonna be able to get boiling oil, so I sent Rowley up to his house to fill some thermoses with hot chocolate.

The homeschooled kids went out and collected icicles to stick into the wall, and the duplex kids threw together some snowmen to make it seem like there were more of us than there actually WERE.

And when the Lower Surrey Street kids came BACK, we were READY for them.

When those guys saw our WALL, they didn't know what to DO.

And when they got CLOSER, we hit them with everything we had.

Those guys didn't stand a CHANCE. We sent them running back down the hill, and we celebrated our victory.

But we celebrated too SOON. Ten minutes later, the Lower Surrey Street kids were BACK.

And this time they were armed to the TEETH.

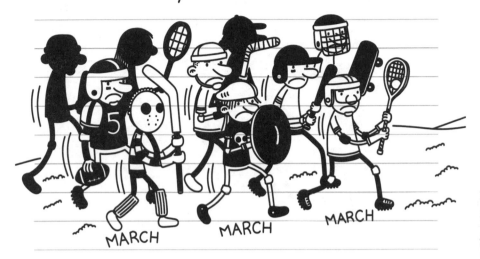

MARCH   MARCH   MARCH

Most of them were wearing sports gear to protect themselves from our snowballs. And the moment I knew this wasn't gonna be an easy fight was when one of them threw a HOCKEY STICK.

THWOK

But still WE were the ones with the WALL, and we had the higher ground.

So we unleashed another round of snowballs.

We held them off for a while, but those guys
had some surprises up their sleeves. They hit us
with a round of Sloppy Specials, which we were
TOTALLY unprepared for.

If the Lower Surrey Street kids had Sloppy
Specials, that meant Mitchell Pickett was playing
both SIDES.

But we'd have to deal with him LATER, because now we had a NEW problem.

It turned out the Sloppy Specials were just a distraction to draw our attention away from the NEXT wave of attack, which was coming at us FAST.

We hit the kids carrying ladders with snowballs, but before we knew it, they'd planted their ladders at the base of the wall and had started climbing their way UP it.

But Rowley came back with the hot chocolate just in the nick of time.

We emptied the thermoses out on the kids scaling the wall. Unfortunately, Rowley hadn't added any WATER to the hot chocolate mix, so all it did was ANNOY them.

I thought those guys were about to take control of the wall, but then Latricia Hooks and Speed Bump saved the day by dumping trash cans full of SLUSH on them.

We didn't have a second to celebrate, though, because the Lower Surrey Street kids were already launching their next attack.

Half the fifth-grade football team lives at the bottom of the hill, and they tried to take down the wall with brute FORCE.

But the wall held UP, and those guys wore themselves out with the effort.

By now, EVERYONE was tired. The sun was out, and it was actually starting to get WARM. I really wished I hadn't worn my thermal underwear, because I was ROASTING with those extra layers.

The Lower Surrey Street kids kept coming at us, and we kept driving them BACK. And after a while, NOBODY had the energy to keep fighting.

Finally, the other team turned around and went back home. At first we thought that meant we had WON. But those guys weren't giving up. They were just REFUELING.

By now it was lunchtime, and the kids at the bottom of the hill came back outside with sandwiches and snacks.

And when some kid started handing out JUICE BOXES, it was a little hard to watch.

We were all pretty thirsty on the wall, and it was only getting HOTTER.

Some kids started sucking on SNOWBALLS to stay hydrated, and they got through half of our stockpile before the rest of us realized what was happening.

We did an inventory of what we had left, and we knew we didn't have enough to fight off a major assault. So we split our remaining snowballs into thirds and put Anthony Denard in charge of protecting them.

We kept waiting for the next attack from the Lower Surrey Street kids, but it never came.

After a while we realized their strategy was to wait us out until we CRACKED, and then take our wall without a fight.

Pervis Gentry was the first one on our side to break. He hadn't even had BREAKFAST this morning, so the sight of all those sandwich crusts lying on the ground made him CRAZY.

He climbed over the wall and ran down the hill, and that was the last any of us saw of him.

But the REST of us hill kids kept it together. Three HOURS went by, but the Lower Surrey Street kids weren't BUDGING.

In fact, they looked like they were settling in for the NIGHT.

A few of them had strung extension cords to their houses, so now they had ELECTRICITY. And we could see the glow of their TV sets from where WE were.

Things were going from bad to worse on the wall. A lot of the younger kids were tired and hungry and wanted to go HOME. And I couldn't blame them, because by now, it was DINNERTIME.

Jacob Hoff said he was supposed to have a clarinet lesson at six o'clock, and if he missed it his parents would be mad. And the rest of us could understand that kind of thing.

Jacob's house was just a few doors down, and we told him if he made a run for it, we'd give him COVER. He promised that the second his clarinet lesson was over, he'd come back to the wall with his coat pockets stuffed with granola bars and fruit chews.

That got everybody pretty excited, and we helped Jacob over the wall. Sure enough, as soon as he touched down on the other side, the Lower Surrey Street kids opened fire on him. But we fired BACK and got Jacob to his front door safely.

It turned out it was a wasted effort, though. The thing about the clarinet lesson was just an excuse to go home, and when we saw Jacob in his bedroom window, we knew he was never coming back with those SNACKS.

After that, the mood inside the wall was really GRIM. Some kids were crying, and I didn't see how we could hold out much longer.

The Lower Surrey Street kids must've known they had us on the ropes, because that's when they launched paper airplanes into our fort with NOTES written on them.

SURRENDER NOW AND YOU CAN LEAVE UNHARMED.

That was too much for some kids to take. Even Baby Gibson seemed shaken up, so I guess now we know he can READ.

A few minutes later, a kid came running toward us from between a couple of houses to the right of our fort, and we got ready to pelt him with a round of snowballs.

But somebody RECOGNIZED the kid, and we held our fire. It was TREVOR NIX, who used to live on the hill.

Trevor was out of breath, and could barely get his words out. So we pulled him up onto the wall and waited for him to calm down.

After Trevor got himself together, he told us what was going on. He said the Lower Surrey Street kids had been holding him CAPTIVE, but he managed to ESCAPE.

Trevor said those guys were planning something really BAD, and he wanted to tell us before it was too LATE.

He said the Lower Surrey Street kids were creating a HUGE stockpile of snowballs, and when it got dark they were gonna launch a full-scale attack. But that wasn't even the WORST part.

Those guys were making their snowballs in the GUZMANS' yard, and that's the place with all the DOGS. So that meant they were using YELLOW SNOW and who knows what ELSE.

Everyone was pretty mad about what the Lower Surrey Street kids were planning, but we were glad Trevor gave us the heads-up. We told him that from now on, he could sled on our hill ANY time.

We agreed we couldn't just sit there and wait for the attack, so we started working on a PLAN. Half of us would sneak down the hill and launch a SURPRISE attack on the kids making snowballs in the Guzmans' yard. The OTHER half would stay back to protect the fort. We sketched the plan into the snow with a stick to make sure we were all on the same page.

ATTACK
TEAM

WALL

GUZMANS'
YARD

Me and Rowley wanted to be a part of the
ACTION, so we chose to be on the sneak attack
team. Our group loaded up a few sleds with all the
snowballs we had left, and we slipped over the
back wall and between some houses.

It was getting dark now, so we knew those guys wouldn't be able to see us coming.

When we got to the Guzmans' backyard, we stopped to scope out the scene. Sure enough, there was a big group of kids making snowballs out front behind a rock wall.

When Baby Gibson gave the signal, we launched our attack.

FLING

But the other guys didn't even FLINCH when we hit them. And as we got closer, we realized it was all just a TRICK.

The Lower Surrey Street kids had created DECOYS to split us up, which meant we'd been double-crossed by TREVOR NIX. We rushed back to the wall, but by then it was already too LATE.

The wall was in RUINS, and we were out of
ammo. It looked really bad for us hill kids, but
then something happened that gave us HOPE.

A group of kids was marching up the hill toward
us, and when they got closer I realized it was
the SAFETY PATROLS. For a brief second, I
thought they were there to SAVE us.

But they weren't there to help ANYONE. They
were there for REVENGE.

Usually, the Safety Patrols aren't allowed to
throw snowballs, but today was a SUNDAY. And
that meant they were free to do whatever they
WANTED.

Half the girls on the Safety Patrols are on the SOFTBALL team, and anybody who says girls can't throw hard doesn't know what they're TALKING about.

The battle turned into the Surrey Street kids versus the Safety Patrols, and we outnumbered them two to one. But then half the girls on our street switched SIDES, and it got really confusing.

In the middle of all this, ANOTHER group came down from the TOP of the hill. It was the WHIRLEY STREET kids, who must've gotten kicked off the golf course and came to sled on our street. And once THEY got into the mix, it was just a total FREE-FOR-ALL.

Just when things couldn't get any CRAZIER, a terrifying sound cut through the air, and everyone stopped to figure out what it WAS. The only ones on the street who knew for SURE were me and Rowley.

AROOOOOOoOOOOOOOO

Then the MINGO kids started pouring out of the woods, looking like they'd just woken up from a three-month NAP.

AROOOOOOOOO

The last Mingo to emerge was MECKLEY. He was carrying something on top of a STICK, and at first I couldn't tell what it was. But when he got CLOSER, I realized it was MR. MORSELS.

Meckley wasn't wearing his BELT, which I thought was strange. But seeing that made me remember something, and I reached into my coat pocket and pulled out something cold and metal.

When me and Rowley were in the Mingos' camp,
I must've put the belt buckle in my pocket
without even REALIZING it. And now I was in
a panic, because that meant Meckley Mingo was
coming for ME.

But the only thing kids in my town hate more than
each OTHER is the MINGOS. So when the
Mingos charged, everyone turned to FACE them.

Well, everyone except ME. At that point I'd
had ENOUGH.

When the Mingos came at us, I looked for a good
place to HIDE.

There was a big hole in a collapsed section of the wall, so I dove inside, and Rowley was right behind me. The battle raged all around us, and I didn't see how we were gonna get out of this one ALIVE.

Rowley didn't think we were gonna make it, either. He told me that if I survived but he DIDN'T, I could have all of his video games.

I patted myself down to see if I had a pen so he could put that in WRITING, but all I had on me was that stupid belt buckle.

It didn't matter anyway, because five seconds later the ground started shaking, and it felt like we were in an EARTHQUAKE.

I thought we were gonna be buried ALIVE, and all I could think of is how the two of us were gonna end up in a MUSEUM after they dug us out in a couple thousand years.

CHILDREN
21ST CENTURY

But then the ground stopped shaking, and after a few seconds we popped our heads out of our hiding spot to see what was happening.

The snowplow was three-quarters of the way up the street, mowing through everything in its path. And I don't know if the snowplow driver couldn't SEE the kids in the road or just didn't CARE.

SPLOSH

By now, the snow was melting, and everything was turning to SLUSH. And once the plow left our street, it was QUIET.

The crazy thing is, now that the street was plowed, there wasn't really anything left to FIGHT over, so everyone picked themselves up and went back HOME. Even the Mingo kids went back to where they came from.

And the truth is, I couldn't really remember what we were all fighting over to BEGIN with.

Friday
We've been back at school for a week, and it's warmed up a LOT in the past few days. I don't want to curse it or anything, but I think we might've seen the last of the cold weather.

So I'm not really worried about the PIG anymore. In fact, he's probably somewhere warm by now, having the time of his life.

There's still some snow on the ground in my neighborhood, so Mitchell Pickett's been enjoying the snowmobile he bought with all the money he made this winter.

So anybody who says that war doesn't PAY should think AGAIN.

Mitchell's not the ONLY one who made out, though. Trevor Nix has been playing hockey down at the bottom of the hill with the Lower Surrey Street kids every day after school. So I guess that's what you get for being a TRAITOR.

But I'm not gonna complain. I'm just glad I made it through the winter without getting myself KILLED.

The thing I learned about myself is that I'm just not the HERO type. Trust me, I'm glad there are people like that out there, but the world needs guys like ME, too.

Because if human beings are still around 500 million years from now, it's gonna be thanks to the Greg Heffleys of the world who figured out a way to SURVIVE.

ACKNOWLEDGMENTS

Thanks to everyone at Abrams, especially Charlie Kochman, who makes every book better. Big thanks to Michael Jacobs, Andrew Smith, Chad W. Beckerman, Liz Fithian, Hallie Patterson, Steve Tager, Melanie Chang, Mary O'Mara, Alison Gervais, and Elisa Garcia. Thanks also to Susan Van Metre and Steve Roman.

Thanks to the great Wimpy Kid team: Shaelyn Germain, Anna Cesary, and Vanessa Jedrej. Thanks to Deb Sundin and the staff at An Unlikely Story.

Thanks to Rich Carr and Andrea Lucey for your support and friendship. Thanks to Paul Sennott for all your help. Thanks to Sylvie Rabineau and Keith Fleer for everything you do for me.

Thanks to Jess Brallier for your mentorship and for getting me started as an author.

ABOUT THE AUTHOR

Jeff Kinney is a #1 *New York Times* bestselling author and a six-time Nickelodeon Kids' Choice Award winner for Favorite Book. Jeff has been named one of *Time* magazine's 100 Most Influential People in the World. He is also the creator of Poptropica, which was named one of *Time*'s 50 Best Websites. He spent his childhood in the Washington, D.C., area and moved to New England in 1995. Jeff lives with his wife and two sons in Massachusetts, where they own a bookstore, An Unlikely Story.